This is a Parragon Publishing book
First published in 2006

Parragon Publishing
Queen Street House
4 Queen Street
Bath, BA1 1HE, UK

ISBN 1-40547-451-3
Printed in China

Soccer Star

Written by Moira Butterfield

Illustrated by Richard Watson

Joe loved soccer. He always cheered for his favorite team on TV, and he had a poster on his bedroom wall showing their top player wearing his champion's medal.

Joe often dreamed of scoring the most fantastic goal ever and winning a big match just like his hero.

Then, one day at school, Joe's teacher made an announcement:
"We are going to be in a soccer tournament with a lot of other schools," she said. "Come to practice tomorrow if you want to be in the team."

At recess, Joe and his friends talked about the tournament.
"You'll be really good, Joe. You love soccer," said his friend Tom.
"We all think you'll be the best player, Joe. You're soccer mad,"
added his friend, Sam.

Joe began to feel worried.
He'd never been on a real
soccer team before.

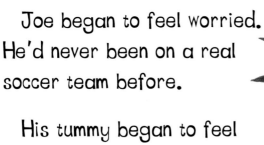

His tummy began to feel
funny, as if there were a lot
of tiny butterflies fluttering
around inside it.

That day, Joe's mom picked him up from school.
"We're going over to Grandpa's house for dinner,"
she said. But Joe wasn't really listening.
He was too busy thinking about the soccer
practice and imagining what might happen.

"What if I kick the ball the wrong way and break a school window?" he thought to himself.

"Or I might fall on my face in the mud..."

"...or my shorts might fall down!"

Now, he was so worried it felt as if the butterflies in his tummy were doing somersaults and cartwheels.

"You look worried about something. Can I help?" Grandpa asked when Joe arrived at his house. Joe told him about the new soccer team and said he felt a bit nervous.

"Well, I know how you feel. I used to play soccer when I was younger," Grandpa said smiling. "Look. I'll show you."

Grandpa brought out an old photo album to show Joe. Inside there were a lot of photographs of soccer players with funny hairstyles and baggy shorts.

"This is me," said Grandpa, pointing to a photo.

"Grandpa! You had the longest shorts in the team," laughed Joe. The laughing made him feel a bit happier.

As Grandpa flicked through the old photo album something slipped out from between the pages. It was shiny and round and hung on a piece of faded ribbon.

Joe took a closer look.
He thought it looked really special.

"Wow! It looks like a winner's medal!" Joe cried.
"Is it yours, Grandpa?"

"Oh, I forgot about that old thing," Grandpa smiled.
"You can have it if you like."

Joe was thrilled. He took the precious medal home with him.

"It's just like the one on my soccer poster. I'm sure it will bring me luck," he thought. He went to bed that night with the medal under his pillow.

The next day, Joe went to the soccer practice at school.
He wore the lucky medal under his T-shirt.

"Great, Joe," his friends cried as he took the ball around
one player and then another.

"Good pass, Joe!" his teacher called out as Joe slipped the
ball to Tom to score a goal.

"Well done, Joe. You're on the team," his teacher told him.

"Yes!" Joe exclaimed, and he touched the medal hanging secretly around his neck. He was sure it had brought him luck.

At last, the day of the tournament arrived. Joe's grandpa came to see him play.

When Joe saw all the other teams his tummy butterflies came back. In the first match, he didn't score. Luckily, somebody else did, and the team won 1-0.

The second match was quite hard, and because he had to try his best, he began to forget about how he felt inside.

This time he scored, and his team won 2-0.

There was one more match before the final, and by now Joe had completely forgotten his butterflies. He passed to Tom, and Tom scored the winning goal!

"We're in the final!" Joe cried, and he went to touch his lucky medal. The ribbon around his neck was empty. The medal had fallen off!

Joe looked around wildly. He couldn't see the medal anywhere, and the final was about to start.

The butterflies came rushing back. The players on the other team looked HUGE.

"What are you looking at?" their goalkeeper grunted at him.

"Er...um...," Joe stuttered. Then, the referee blew his whistle, and the game began!

Joe was still in a panic. While he was worrying, a player from the other side took the ball off him and raced away toward the goal. Luckily, Sam made a great save, but Joe knew he'd nearly given a goal away.

It was 0-0 for ages. Joe couldn't seem to concentrate.

Dimly in the background, Joe heard his grandpa shouting.

"Come on, Joe!"

Tom passed the ball to Joe. He looked up toward the goal and began to dribble the ball. He made it around a defender, but then, the big goalkeeper stared at him and began to move forward.

Joe knew this was his chance to score, but the thought made his legs suddenly feel heavy. He felt as if he was going to turn into a statue.

Then, he saw something shiny out of the corner of his eye.
It was sitting in the grass near the goalposts.
  "That's my lucky medal!" he gasped.
  The medal glittered, and Joe knew what he had to do.
He swung his foot back, kicked as hard as he could, and...

"GOAL!"

The crowd cheered. In the next few seconds, the referee blew his whistle to end the match.

"You scored! You're great!" Joe's friends cried,
punching the air and chanting:
    "We won the cup! We won the cup!"

Joe bent down and picked up the medal.
"Thank goodness I found you," he whispered.

Joe ran over to his grandpa.

"Thanks Grandpa. I couldn't have done it without your lucky soccer medal," he said.

"Oh, that," he nodded. "I remember where I won it now. I came first in a funny faces contest on vacation."

"Oh, but it's definitely a lucky medal. It helped me win," Joe insisted.

Grandpa smiled and shook his head.

"The medal didn't do it. YOU did it! Perhaps it helped make you feel less worried, but you won the cup because you tried your best. Now, go and get your own medal. You deserve it!"

Grandpa had taken a lot of photos of Joe getting his own winner's medal.

"Here is a photo to put up in your bedroom, next to that poster of your hero," said Grandpa.

"You can have your funny faces medal back, Grandpa. I still think it might be lucky," Joe insisted.

"Oh, I don't think so," Grandpa began, and then he stopped and thought for a moment.

"Well, I suppose if something makes you feel lucky, then it is special," he smiled.

"And we are special, Grandpa. We are the champions!" Joe exclaimed grinning.